This book is a work of fiction. Any references to historical events, real people, or real places are used fictitiously. Other names, characters, places, and events are products of the author's imagination, and any resemblance to actual events or places or persons, living or dead, is entirely coincidental.

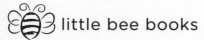 little bee books

An imprint of Bonnier Publishing USA
251 Park Avenue South, New York, NY 10010
Copyright © 2017 by Bonnier Publishing USA
All rights reserved, including the right of
reproduction in whole or in part in any form.
LITTLE BEE BOOKS is a registered trademark of Bonnier Publishing USA,
and associated colophon is a trademark of Bonnier Publishing USA.
Manufactured in the United States of America LB 0917
ISBN: 978-1-4998-0466-9 (hc)
First Edition 10 9 8 7 6 5 4 3 2 1
ISBN: 978-1-4998-0465-2 (pbk)
First Edition 10 9 8 7 6 5 4 3 2 1

Library of Congress Cataloging-in-Publication Data
Names: Pearl, Alexa, author. | Sordo, Paco, illustrator.
Title: Wings for Wyatt / by Alexa Pearl; illustrated by Paco Sordo.
Description: First edition. | New York, NY: Little Bee Books, [2017] | Series: Tales of Sasha;
#6 | Summary: During a visit home, everyone treats Sasha differently except her best friend,
Wyatt, so she tries to find a way for him to fly with her to the Island of Royal Flying Horses.
Identifiers: LCCN 2017023556 | Subjects: | CYAC: Best friends—Fiction. | Friendship—Fiction.
| Horses—Fiction. | Animals, Mythical—Fiction. | Princesses—Fiction. | Family life—Fiction.
| BISAC: JUVENILE FICTION / Readers / Chapter Books. | JUVENILE FICTION / Animals /
Horses. | JUVENILE FICTION / Animals / Mythical. | Classification: LCC PZ7.1.P425 Win 2017
| DDC [Fic]—dc23
LC record available at https://lccn.loc.gov/2017023556

littlebeebooks.com
bonnierpublishingusa.com

Tales of
SASHA

Wings for Wyatt

by Alexa Pearl
illustrated by Paco Sordo

little bee books

Contents

Lucky Charm

"I'm not going," said Sasha. Her words echoed across the sky.

She landed on the ground and the royal flying horses followed and gathered around her.

Sapphire circled Sasha. Her blue coat gleamed in the sun, and she frowned. "What?"

Sasha flapped her wings quickly. She was nervous. Sapphire ruled the flying horses. No one ever refused her orders. Until now.

"I'm not going to the Royal Island," Sasha said, trying to make her voice sound strong, even though her knees wobbled. "I can't."

Sapphire's bright blue eyes narrowed. "Why not?"

"I miss my family," Sasha said with a gulp. "It's been so long since I've seen them."

Sapphire's frown went away. Her voice softened. "We're your family, too. Your flying family."

"You're our Lost Princess," added Sasha's friend Kimani. "We need you."

Sasha's head was spinning. So much had happened so fast.

Only a little while ago, she was living in Verdant Valley with her parents and two sisters. She had known she was different than the other horses, but she couldn't figure out how. Then, one day, wings had popped out of her back. She could fly!

Sasha was a flying horse.

Soon she learned that other flying horses lived in Crystal Cove. Sasha traveled to meet them. She discovered she was their Lost Princess! They had left her with a family of regular horses when she was a baby. They had wanted to keep their princess safe from the plant pixies.

Now the plant pixies and the flying horses were friends thanks to Sasha. She'd fixed everything with her special Lost Princess powers. Sapphire wanted Sasha to go to the Royal Island to meet someone important. She wouldn't tell Sasha who it was yet.

Sasha was curious, but . . . the island was far away out in the sea.

Sasha missed her family in Verdant Valley. She missed her friends. She missed the green fields and even her lessons at school.

Sasha wanted to help the flying horses. She also wanted to give her mom a big nuzzle.

"I don't know what to do," Sasha said to Sapphire. "I have two families now."

"The more family, the more love."
Sapphire looked to the sky. "The best
time to fly to the island is when a rainbow
fills the sky. The sun will shine today and
tomorrow. Then the rain and the rainbow
will come. You can go to Verdant Valley
before going to the island."

"Thank you!" cried Sasha. She
promised Sapphire she'd go to the island
as soon as the rainbow appeared.

"I can't believe she's letting you
go." Kimani looked shocked.
Sapphire never changed
her mind.

"We're so lucky Sasha came back to us." Sapphire untied a long, thin, velvet ribbon with a small gold star attached to it from around her tail.

"What is that?" asked Sasha.

"A lucky star," Sapphire said, tying it to Sasha's gray tail.

"Oh, I want a lucky star, too," cried Kimani.

"This star brings luck *only* when worn by a royal horse, like Sasha," said Sapphire.

"Why do I need luck?" asked Sasha.

"Flying around the rainbow to the island is tricky." Sapphire touched the star. "This lucky star will keep you safe. Make sure you travel with it."

Sasha had never had a lucky charm before. She swished her tail to show it to Kimani.

"It's so sparkly!" said Kimani. She smiled at Sasha.

"Are you ready?" asked Sapphire.

"I am!" Sasha said goodbye to all the flying horses. Then she opened her wings wide and soared across the sky. She was going home.

CHAPTER 2

The Princess Is Back

Sasha dipped below the clouds. The wind ruffled her mane as she picked up speed. She joined a flock of birds heading south. Sasha loved to run and jump, but flying was a hundred million times more fun.

As she flew, she watched the ground far below her.

She saw the big lake.

She saw the field of neon flowers.

She saw the big trees of the forest.

Then she saw the green fields of Verdant Valley.

"Have a good trip! Stay warm!" she called to the birds. She soared in for a landing.

Bam!

Her hoofs hit the ground hard. Clumps of dirt and grass sprayed into the air.

She skidded to a shaky stop—right in front of a very surprised sheep.

"Where did you come from?" The sheep asked, looking from Sasha to the sky above. In Verdant Valley, horses didn't fly.

Sasha used her tail to brush the dirt off the sheep. "Sorry about your wool. Landing isn't my thing."

"Is that you?"

"She's back!"

"Zara! Poppy!" Sasha galloped toward her two older sisters.

They frolicked in the field, happy to see her. They wanted to know all about her adventures in Crystal Cove.

Sasha beamed. Before Sasha had her wings, Zara and Poppy had been a team, and Sasha had to scramble for their attention. She liked being in the spotlight now.

Her mom and dad hurried over. They nuzzled her. Sasha nuzzled them back.

Horses from her class at school cantered over and chanted her name. Caleb, her old teacher, gave her a salute. She was the star.

Sasha smiled, but her eyes searched the crowd. Where was Wyatt?

Twinkle came up to Sasha—and curtsied!

"What's with the curtsy?" Sasha giggled. Twinkle and Sasha had been school friends since they were foals. Why was Twinkle suddenly acting so polite?

"You're a princess now. May I touch your wings?"

Poppy jumped in between them.
"Sorry, Twinkle. No touching."

"But—" Sasha didn't care if her wings
were touched.

"We need to let her eat," Zara told
Twinkle and the gathering crowd. Zara
and Poppy led her to their family's
cottonwood tree.

Sasha looked back. All the horses waved their tails at her.

All the horses except for Wyatt. Where was her best friend?

Her mother led Sasha to a huge hollowed-out log filled with applesauce and honey. "The other horse families made this for you."

"Yum!" Sasha slurped a huge mouthful. "Come on! Everyone have some, too— or I'll eat it all."

No one moved. "It's just for you," said Poppy.

"*What?!*" Sasha was confused. Applesauce was Poppy's favorite.

"It has your name on it." Poppy pointed to the tag attached to the log:

Only for Sasha
the flying princess

"Are you kidding? You can share my food. Nothing has changed."

Yet everything had changed. She was given the best spot to rest and now the best foods to eat. The horses in the herd brought her cool water to drink and fanned her with their tails. Her sisters didn't even tease her like they used to.

Sasha sighed. All this special treatment was . . . weird.

She wanted to run and have fun. She needed her best friend to play with her. Where was Wyatt?

A Race to the Top

"Watcha know, Wyatt-o?!" Sasha called. She'd found him at the bottom of Mystic Mountain.

Wyatt laughed. "That's a ridiculous greeting."

"It's not my best rhyme," agreed Sasha. "How about: Everyone get quiet for Wyatt!"

"That's better." Wyatt chewed loudly. His cheeks bulged with wildflowers.

"You weren't in the field when I landed," said Sasha. "Why not?"

"Too many horses." He took a bite out of a daisy.

"Didn't you want to hear about my adventures?"

"Are you forgetting I was the first to see you fly? I went with you to Crystal Cove. I battled the plant pixies." Wyatt smirked. "I know how it *all* went down, remember?"

"You do," Sasha agreed. Wyatt had been by her side, but he'd come back to Verdant Valley before she had.

"Did you miss me?" she asked a little sadly. She'd missed him.

"Nah," he teased. "More wildflowers for me with you gone."

"Well, I'm back now. Race you to the top!" Sasha took off up the mountain.

Wyatt gave chase. They leaped over streams. They darted around rocks. They ran neck and neck.

Sasha was relieved. Wyatt didn't care that she could fly or that she was a princess. Everything was the same with him. They were still better-than-best friends.

On the mountaintop, they spotted the wildflowers. Wyatt put on a burst of speed.

Sasha slowed a teeny, tiny bit, letting Wyatt get there first. Sometimes friends did that.

"I won!" He pumped a hoof in the air. "I get the blue cornflowers."

Whenever they raced, the winner always got his or her first choice of flower to eat.

"I'll take the zinnias," said Sasha.

For a few minutes, their chewing was the only noise on the mountain. A hawk made lazy circles in the sky above Verdant Valley. The land beyond the big trees stretched out before them off in the distance.

"You know what? We should set up an obstacle course this weekend. Remember when we did that? We'll make the jumps even higher this time." Wyatt spoke fast, excited by the idea. "Or we could go on a berry hunt. Just you and me."

"I can't." She told him about going to the Royal Island out in the ocean.

"That's far away," said Wyatt. "Aren't you scared?"

Sasha showed him the gold star on the ribbon. "This lucky charm will keep me safe."

"Who's on the island?" asked Wyatt. "Is it . . . ?"

He didn't finish. He knew she hoped the King and Queen were on the island. Then she'd finally meet the flying horses who'd given birth to her. But Sasha wouldn't jinx it by saying it out loud. So Wyatt wouldn't either.

"I wish I could see the magical island, too," said Wyatt.

That's when Sasha had the best idea ever. "Come with me."

"How? It's too far to swim, and I can't fly."

Sasha considered this.

There was only one answer. She'd teach Wyatt how to fly. "First, you need a pair of wings."

Wyatt's Wings

"Who am I going to get wings from?" asked Wyatt.

"Not from me!" called a hawk from up in the sky.

"Keep your hooves off my feathers!" warned an owl in a nearby tree.

"Poppy can make them," said Sasha. Her sister had twisted a top hat out of twigs and woven a blanket from moss.

They hurried down the mountain. Poppy was by their family tree.

"Wings shouldn't be hard," said Poppy after hearing their request.

Sasha opened hers. Poppy looked closely at the pale, sparkly feathers. "I'll need something the same shape as a feather."

With her hoof, Poppy drew the shape of the feather-like substitute she'd need in the dirt.

"I know!" cried Sasha. "A leaf is that same shape."

Wyatt pointed up at the wide leaves on a nearby cottonwood tree. "Not those leaves."

"Over there." Sasha showed them a black walnut tree with leaves that looked like feathers.

With tree sap, Poppy glued the leaves Sasha and Wyatt removed from the tree, one on top of the other. By the next morning, Poppy had two enormous leaf wings. She strapped them onto Wyatt's back.

"They feel funny." He twisted himself around to get a better look at them.

"Stop twisting. You're making them go all crooked." Poppy straightened his floppy wings. "Okay. Time to fly."

Wyatt stood in the middle of the field. The sun shone brightly on him.

"Flap the wings!" called Poppy.

"How?" asked Wyatt. "Is there an on button?"

"Of course not." Sasha's wings sprouted from the white patch on her back. She showed him how they flapped up and down.

"Mine don't work like that," said Wyatt.

"Maybe the wings will move when you're in the air," said Poppy. "Jump off something high. How about Mystic Mountain?"

"Seriously?" The mountain reached up into the clouds. "If the wings don't work, I'll *splat*, like a pancake."

Instead, Wyatt climbed onto the big
rock in the field. It wasn't too high off
the ground. "One . . . two . . . three!"
He leaped into the air, and . . .

Oooooof!

He flopped flat onto the grass. "Did I do it? Did I fly? A little?"

"Not a bit," called Poppy.

"But I felt something move on my back. Was it the wings?"

"Oh, no!" Poppy started to laugh. Sasha joined in.

The hot sun had melted the sap and the leaves had come undone. Now they were stuck along the top of Wyatt's back. He looked like a strange stegosaurus!

"This isn't going to work. Your wings are a goopy, prehistoric mess," said Sasha.

"Don't you have a special power that can make me fly?" asked Wyatt.

"I only have two powers. Sparks explode from my tail when I get angry. And I can talk to plant pixies," said Sasha.

Wyatt sighed. It looked like he'd never get to travel to the island with Sasha.

"Wait!" cried Sasha. "The plant pixies *are* the answer."

"How?" asked Poppy.

"Vines shoot out of their wrists," said Sasha. "Their vines are stronger than rope. What if I get a bunch of pixies to tie their vines tightly around Wyatt? Plant pixies ride on the backs on hummingbirds. The hummingbirds will fly while the plant pixies hold onto Wyatt."

"Like I'm a special delivery package," joked Wyatt.

"Maybe it's a bad idea," Sasha continued. "Well, we could—"

Wyatt didn't let her finish. "I say we try it."

Sasha called for any nearby pixies and hummingbirds to come to her.

Special Delivery

Six tiny plant pixies and six hummingbirds flew in. One was Collie, Sasha's pixie friend. They listened to Sasha's instructions.

Four pixies wrapped vines around each of Wyatt's legs. One wrapped vines around his tail. The last pixie, Collie, wrapped vines around his head. The pixies sat on top of their hummingbirds and held on tight.

"Fly as fast as you can," Sasha told the hummingbirds.

The hummingbirds' tiny wings flapped in a furious blur of motion. They huffed and puffed. Their eyes bulged as they tried to lift Wyatt.

Wyatt's hooves rose off the ground. One inch . . . two inches.

He was going up!

"Yes!" cried Sasha.

Plop! Wyatt hit the ground.

The hummingbirds had run out of strength. They tried again, but lifting a horse was way too hard for them.

"There has to be another way." Wyatt refused to give up. "Let's try something else."

"We're running out of time. The rainbow will be in the sky at the end of the day to show me the way to the island," Sasha added.

"I really want to come with you," insisted Wyatt. "We *always* have adventures together."

Sasha promised to keep thinking. "First, let's wash off those sticky leaves in the river."

Other horses were cooling off in the river. Sasha and Wyatt ran into the clear water. Twinkle and another friend, Chester, splashed nearby.

Twinkle turned and splashed Wyatt. Wyatt splashed Twinkle.

Sasha splashed Twinkle, too. Twinkle didn't splash her back. She just smiled at Sasha.

Sasha splashed Chester. He didn't splash back either.

"What's going on?" she asked.

Twinkle and Chester stayed silent. Slowly, she began to understand. No one wanted to splash the flying horse princess. Sasha sighed. This wasn't the way home was supposed to be.

Whap!

Wyatt slapped the water with his tail, sending a wave crashing over her.

Sasha had never been so happy.

"Watch out!" She slapped her tail to drench him. Soon Twinkle and Chester joined in. They splashed Sasha. She splashed them back. Water sprayed everywhere!

Wyatt had made everything okay again.

"Lunchtime," Wyatt called. He stood on the riverbank, drying his white coat in the sun.

Sasha shook out her wet mane and followed him to the shade of her family's cottonwood tree where her family was gathered. Red pears rested on a plaid blanket. She gave her mother a big nuzzle of thanks, then bit into a juicy pear.

Suddenly, Wyatt called out. "Your lucky charm! Where is it?"

"What do you mean?" Sasha whirled about, trying to see her tail.

"It's not there," reported Wyatt. "The ribbon must have come undone!"

"Go back to the river," said her mother. "It must have slipped off."

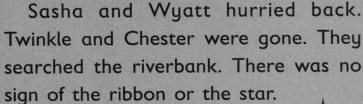

Sasha and Wyatt hurried back. Twinkle and Chester were gone. They searched the riverbank. There was no sign of the ribbon or the star.

Sasha stepped into the water. She felt around the muddy bottom with her hooves.

She found a stone.

She found a turtle.

This was taking way too long.

Sasha plunged her head beneath the surface. Water rushed by, as the current traveled downstream. A curious catfish swam around her face.

She scanned the murky bottom—and spotted a ribbon!

She grabbed it with her teeth. She jerked her head out of the water to celebrate.

Yuck! A long strand of seaweed hung from her mouth. Sasha spat it out. That wasn't the ribbon.

As she watched the water swirl and flow, she had the sinking feeling that her lucky charm had washed away.

CHAPTER 6

Twice as Much Luck

"I can't believe I lost Sapphire's lucky star right when I have to fly through the rainbow," said Sasha.

"Will you be okay without it?" Wyatt sounded concerned.

Sasha shrugged. "Sapphire said the flight was tricky."

"Maybe you shouldn't go. What if something bad happens if you don't have the lucky charm?"

"I'm scared Sapphire will be upset," said Sasha.

"Because you lost the star or because you aren't going to the island?"

"Both."

"Let's keep looking," said Wyatt. "Maybe it's in the field."

Sasha shivered from being in the water so long. She climbed out.

Whoa! Her hooves slipped on the muddy riverbank. She tumbled backward into the water.

"Are you okay?" Wyatt scrambled to help her up.

"Just wet."

"Oh, no," said Wyatt. "You're having bad luck already."

"Really?" Sasha groaned. "I don't want *bad* luck."

Sasha followed Wyatt into the field. Wyatt searched under the black walnut tree. Still no charm.

Sasha called out for Collie. Collie flew in on Lucia, her special hummingbird. Sasha had Collie write a tiny note to deliver to Kimani.

Sasha watched Collie fly off on Lucia. She'd bring the note to Kimani.

"What's wrong?" Zara hurried over. "You and Wyatt both look sad."

"Is it the wings? I can try to make a new pair," said Poppy, now joining them. "Maybe I'll use tree bark this time."

"It's not that." Sasha told them about the missing charm. She needed good luck to fly through the rainbow.

Zara walked up and down the field. She pushed her nose through the tall grass like a vacuum cleaner. "Maybe there's another way to get luck." Zara nosed around more, then cried out, "Found one!"

She held up a four-leaf clover.
"Four-leaf clovers are very lucky."
Zara tucked it behind Sasha's ear.

"I have something lucky, too." Poppy
cantered away. She came back with a
gray flannel square of fabric.

"Your blankie bit?" Sasha couldn't believe her sister would give her this. She slept with the last piece of her foal blanket every night.

"It always brings me luck." Poppy tucked the blankie square behind Sasha's other ear. "You can borrow it."

Sasha nuzzled her sisters with thanks.

"With the clover and the blankie, I'll have twice as much luck. I can fly around the rainbow tonight."

"When will you leave?" Zara asked.

Sasha looked up. Gray clouds floated in, threatening rain. After the rain, a rainbow should appear. "Pretty soon, I think."

"We'd better tell Mom and Dad." Poppy and Zara headed off.

Sasha stood under the tree. *Plop! Plop! Plop!*

"Ow!" Out of nowhere, dozens of small, hard walnuts clattered down on Sasha. They stung as they bounced off her back.

She ducked her head. Were the clouds raining walnuts instead of water?

"What happened?" Wyatt raced over to her.

"All the nuts fell from the tree," whispered Sasha.

Wyatt's eyes grew wide. They both had heard the stories growing up. Something like that only happens for one reason—because someone was carrying bad luck.

"Oh, no! I've become cursed with bad luck!" cried Sasha.

"I guess Zara's clover and Poppy's blankie didn't stop it," Wyatt told her.

"I must find Sapphire's charm. That's the only way to fix this. Let's search the river again," said Sasha.

"Not without me!"

Sasha looked around the empty field.
Who said that?
"Up here!"

Sasha lifted her eyes to the sky. Kimani's purple wings shimmered and her braided tail bounced as she circled the clouds. Kimani soared in for a graceful landing. She didn't kick up a single blade of grass. "Collie gave me your note."

"Everything's going wrong," Sasha told her. "I lost the charm, and now I've become bad luck."

"You? Bad luck?" Kimani looked confused. "The charm brings good luck, but *not* having it shouldn't bring bad luck."

"It did for me." Sasha told her about slipping on the mud and the tree throwing its walnuts.

"Throwing?" Kimani laughed. "Even from up in the sky, I saw Wyatt shaking the tree. *He* made the walnuts fall."

"What?" cried Sasha. "Wyatt, was it really you?"

Wyatt's ears went flat. "I'm sorry. I wanted you to think you had bad luck, even with the double luck from the clover and blankie."

Sasha stared thoughtfully at Wyatt.
Then she walked toward the river.

"Sasha, wait!" Wyatt called as he
and Kimani hurried after her.

Sasha didn't stop until she got to a low stone wall. She pushed one stone aside. Wyatt kept his treasures inside the hollow nook. They were such good friends that it hadn't taken Sasha long to figure out what he'd done.

Inside, she found:

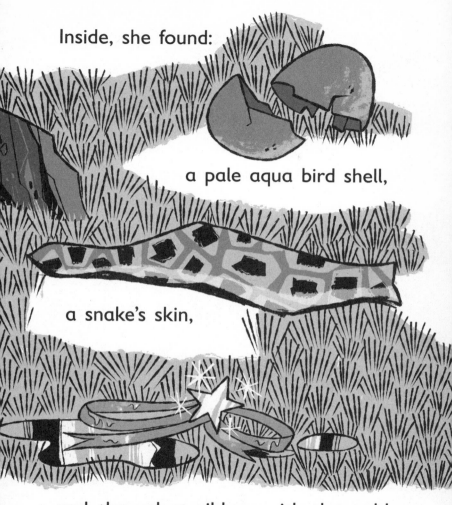

a pale aqua bird shell,

a snake's skin,

and the velvet ribbon with the gold star charm!

"My good luck charm!" Sasha lifted up the wet ribbon with her teeth.

"I saw it fall off while you were in the river," Wyatt said softly.

"You hid it from me. You made me think it was gone forever," said Sasha.

"Why did you take away Sasha's good luck charm?" asked Kimani. "I thought you were her best friend."

"I am," said Wyatt. "That's why I took it."

CHAPTER 8

The Hammock

"I don't understand," Sasha said as Kimani tied the ribbon to her tail again.

"You were going to fly off to the island," Wyatt told Sasha. "I know you're a princess and you have to help the flying horses, but I miss having my best friend around."

"Did you hope she'd stay here if she didn't have the good luck charm?" asked Kimani. "Is that why you hid it?"

Wyatt nodded.

"But you didn't even say you missed me the last time I was gone," said Sasha.

"Well . . . I thought you knew." Wyatt looked embarrassed. "I'm sorry. It seemed like a good idea. I wanted to go with you, too."

Sasha sighed. She wished Wyatt hadn't tried to trick her, but she understood that he felt left out. "If only we could figure out how to get you to fly," she said.

"It'll take too long to try to make new wings or invent some other contraption." Wyatt stuck out his tongue to catch the first raindrops. "It's raining already."

Sasha paced back and forth. "I wish I were strong enough to carry you."

"That's it! Maybe we can carry Wyatt," said Kimani. "Do you have a large blanket?"

"My mother does." Sasha raced to get the plaid blanket.

Kimani laid it on the ground between them. She had Wyatt lie in the middle of it.

"We'll use it like a hammock." Kimani gathered one end of the blanket and held it tight between her teeth. Sasha did the same on the other side.

The rain began to fall faster. On Kimani's command, they bent their knees, opened their wings, and took off into the sky.

"Wait!" cried Wyatt.

Kimani and Sasha hadn't noticed that Wyatt had slid off! They held an empty blanket between them.

"Oops! Sorry," said Kimani. "That didn't work."

"Tell me about it." Wyatt pointed to his sore rump. He'd fallen a lot lately.

The rain slowed, then stopped. Sunlight peeked out from behind the clouds. Sasha was running out of time.

"Did you find out about the rainbow? Will there be another one if I don't go now?" Sasha asked Kimani.

"I don't know," admitted Kimani. "You told me not to tell Sapphire."

Sasha had to make her choice quickly. Should she go to the island now without Wyatt? Or should she stay in Verdant Valley and hope for another rainbow? And if she stayed, would she ever be able to figure out a way to make Wyatt fly?

Through the Rainbow

Before she could decide, Wyatt had another idea. "I just need a better way to stay on the blanket. It was too slippery the first time. I have to be strapped in."

"Maybe we could use the plant pixies' vines?" asked Sasha.

"Sasha, the rainbow's coming out," warned Kimani. "You need to hurry."

"We can do this." Sasha felt a jolt of excitement. "The hummingbirds weren't strong enough to lift Wyatt, but together, we can do it."

"What are you thinking?" asked Kimani.

"I'll show you." She called for Collie and the other plant pixies. They flew in on their hummingbirds. Sasha had a few pixies climb on her tail and mane, and a few were gathered on Kimani. The plant pixies braided themselves into the horses' hair.

Then they shot out their thick vines. The vines wrapped around Wyatt's body, holding him tightly.

"This feels weird." Wyatt was quickly covered in vines.

The rainbow glimmered in the sky. The time to go was now.

Sasha checked that the ribbon with the lucky charm was attached to her tail.

Then Kimani gave a snort. They bent their knees, spread their wings, and took to the sky.

Wyatt floated up with them! All three horses were in the air!

Flying with Wyatt wasn't hard at all. As long as Sasha and Kimani flew at the same speed, everything would be great.

Sasha smiled widely. Wyatt and Kimani were *both* coming to the island with her! And so were Collie and the other plant pixies.

They were all on their way. Together.
That was the best luck of all.

Sasha flapped her wings faster and
headed toward the rainbow.

Read on for a sneak peek
from the seventh book in the
Tales of Sasha series!

Tales of
SASHA

The Royal Island

by Alexa Pearl

illustrated by Paco Sordo

CHAPTER 1) A Wild Ride

"We found the rainbow!" cheered Sasha.

The rainbow shimmered and glowed in the pale blue sky.

"It's so close. We should fly faster to reach it sooner," said Wyatt.

Kimani laughed. "We? I think you mean Sasha and I should fly faster."

Kimani flapped her purple wings and Sasha flapped her gray wings. Wyatt couldn't flap any wings, because he didn't have wings. He wasn't a flying horse like Sasha and Kimani.

But Wyatt was up in the sky anyway.

The enchanted plant pixies had wrapped their strong vines around Wyatt. The vines held him in a kind of hammock. The tiny pixies grabbed onto Sasha and Kimani's manes, and the flying horses carried Wyatt through the air.

Sasha was proud of her horse-carrying invention.

The three horse friends were on a mission. "We must go around the rainbow to get to the Royal Island," said Sasha.

"Full speed ahead!" cried Wyatt.

"Excuse me . . . full speed?" Kimani's violet eyes twinkled with mischief. "Did you hear him, Sasha?"

"I did." Sasha's gray eyes also twinkled.

Sasha and Kimani put on a burst of speed. A gust of wind washed over their faces. The plant pixies tightened their grip so Wyatt would stay safe in the harness.

A puffy cloud floated in. Sasha and Kimani dipped under it. Then they soared high over the next cloud. Under and over.

"Whoa!" Wyatt grew dizzy with all the swoops and dips. He closed his eyes. Oh, no! That made it much worse. He felt like a kite caught in a hurricane.

"Wyatt's looking a little bit green," Sasha called to Kimani.

"I like green horses," teased Kimani. All flying horses had bright-colored coats. Kimani herself had a purple coat.

"I don't want to be green." Wyatt liked being a white horse. "Slow down, please!"

The rainbow arched across the sky. They flew around it, then slowed.

"Are you okay?" Sasha asked Wyatt.

Wyatt nodded.

Now they were gliding high above the sea. White-tipped waves crashed far below. Looking at them made him even queasier.

"Where's the Royal Island?" asked Sasha.

Below them, the sea stretched on and on to the horizon. There was no island in sight.

Sasha had been sent by Sapphire to meet someone very special on the island. Sapphire ruled the herd of flying horses that lived in Crystal Cove.

Flying horses!

Sasha still couldn't believe it. Up until a couple of weeks ago, she hadn't known flying horses even existed. Sasha had thought she was an ordinary horse. She grazed in the fields. She went to school. Then one day, the white patch on her back began to itch—and wings popped out. Sasha could fly!

That's when the excitement began.

"How do we find the island?" Sasha asked. "I don't know which way to go."

"Special delivery!" boomed a voice behind them. The toucan flew up beside them. "Next time, ask for directions before you go on a long journey."

"Good point," agreed Sasha. "Can you help us?"

The toucan was Sapphire's messenger. With his colorful beak, he handed her a pair of goggles. "Put these on. The words will lead you."

"Thank you," Sasha said as a pixie helped place them on her head.

"Waste no time," warned the toucan. "The horses you are to meet will leave the Royal Island tomorrow night."

"Is it far?" asked Wyatt.

But the toucan had already flown away.